ELI AND THE DIMPLEMEYERS

by Marc Kornblatt • illustrated by Jack Ziegler

Macmillan Publishing Company   New York
Maxwell Macmillan Canada   Toronto
Maxwell Macmillan International   New York   Oxford   Singapore   Sydney

For the Grunes Family

—M. K.

To the memory of Harvey Kurtzman

—J. Z.

Text copyright © 1994 by Marc Kornblatt
Illustrations copyright © 1994 by Jack Ziegler
All rights reserved. No part of this book may be reproduced or transmitted in any form or by any means, electronic or mechanical, including photocopying, recording, or by any information storage and retrieval system, without permission in writing from the Publisher. Macmillan Publishing Company is part of the Maxwell Communication Group of Companies. Macmillan Publishing Company, 866 Third Avenue, New York, NY 10022. Maxwell Macmillan Canada, Inc., 1200 Eglinton Avenue East, Suite 200, Don Mills, Ontario M3C 3N1. First edition. Printed in the United States of America. The text of this book is set in 15 pt. Usherwood Book. The illustrations are rendered in pen and ink and watercolor.
10 9 8 7 6 5 4 3 2 1
Library of Congress Cataloging-in-Publication Data. Kornblatt, Marc. Eli and the Dimplemeyers / by Marc Kornblatt ; illustrated by Jack Ziegler. — 1st ed.   p.   cm. Summary: Some special advice helps Eli remain friends with the highly unusual Dimplemeyer clan without upsetting his own more conventional family. ISBN 0-02-750947-8   [1. Imaginary playmates—Fiction.]   I. Ziegler, Jack, ill.   II. Title.
PZ7.K8373El   1994   [E]—dc20   92-36793

Eli Finkel's friends, the Dimplemeyers, were a most unusual family.

Mr. Donald Dimplemeyer was a tall, tall man with a bald, bald head and gold teeth. In a certain light his smile and head could be blinding.

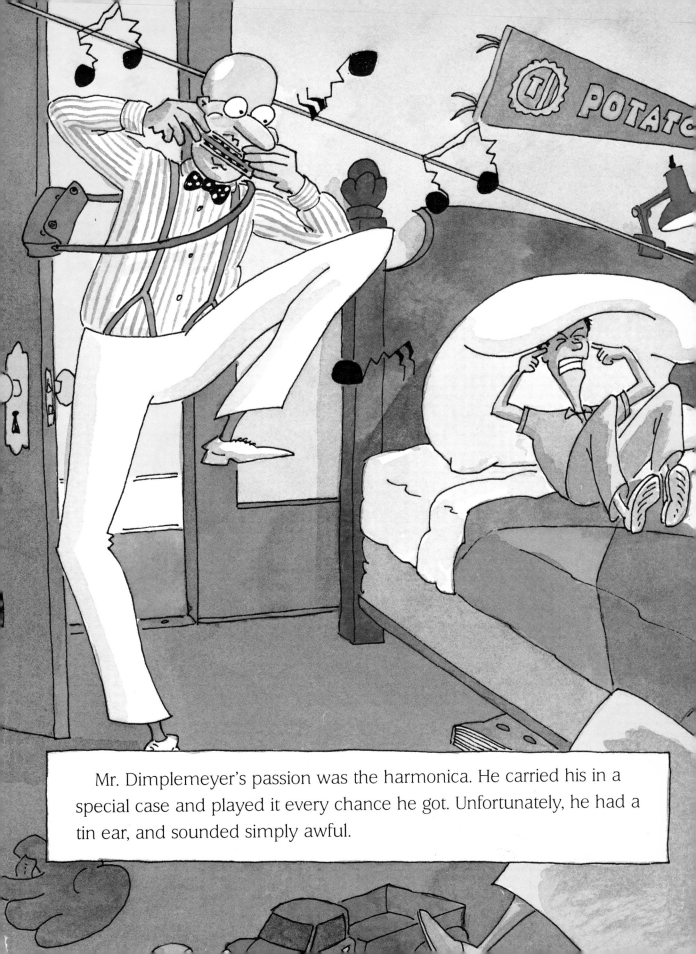

Mr. Dimplemeyer's passion was the harmonica. He carried his in a special case and played it every chance he got. Unfortunately, he had a tin ear, and sounded simply awful.

It was a good thing that in addition to dirt bike racing, his wife Doris adored knitting. She made earmuffs for everyone in the family to spare them from Mr. Dimplemeyer's music.

Their daughter Drusilla, however, refused to wear hers. That's because she had beautiful long red hair, and earmuffs tended to tangle it. To drown out her father, she sang cowboy songs at the top of her lungs.

Drusilla had a lovely voice, but no one ever heard her, since she sang only when her father played his harmonica. And whenever he played, everybody wore earmuffs. Everybody except Drusilla.

The youngest Dimplemeyer—Dalrymple was his name—dreamed of joining the circus and becoming a tightrope walker.

It was a crazy notion, considering that his nickname—Trip—fit him to a tee.

No question about it, the Dimplemeyers were an odd bunch. But what made them truly extraordinary was the fact that Eli was the only person in his family who could actually see them.

Because of this, they needed his constant protection.
Danger lurked everywhere.

One time Eli and his friends were in the den, minding their own business, when Eli's dad came in and almost squashed poor Mrs. Dimplemeyer.

Then there was the day they were playing outside, and Eli's sister Marla, not watching where she was going, nearly broke Trip's neck.

It was exhausting for Eli. To make matters worse, his family didn't like his friends at all.

Mr. Finkel wouldn't let Mr. Dimplemeyer borrow his razor. When Eli asked him why, he said, "Because make-believe people don't have real beards, that's why."

Mrs. Finkel got upset whenever Mrs. Dimplemeyer set foot in the kitchen.

"Eli, where did all our eggs go?" she asked one day.

"Mrs. Dimplemeyer baked a chocolate forest cake."

"That's going to cost a dollar out of your allowance."

Marla wouldn't even discuss the Dimplemeyers with Eli. Every time their name came up she scowled. "Kid," she would say, "you're too weird for words."

Things got so bad that Eli's parents decided to take him to a psychiatrist.

The couch in the psychiatrist's office was firm and very bouncy. Trip thought it made a fine trampoline.

"Tell me about Doris," the psychiatrist asked Eli.

"What?" said Eli.

"Your friend who likes dirt bikes. What's she like?"

"Who?"

"Mrs. Dimplemeyer."

"Huh?"

Conversation was impossible thanks to Trip's bouncing, Mr. Dimplemeyer's harmonica playing, and Drusilla's singing.

"I think you need to consult a hearing specialist," the psychiatrist later told Eli's parents.

That night after dinner, Mr. Finkel followed Eli to his room. "Son," he said, "we're at the end of our rope."

"So is Trip," replied Eli, which was true.

Grandma Bessie was Mr. Finkel's mother. As the oldest member of the Finkel clan she commanded respect. She lived on the other side of Milwaukee from Eli's family, and the next day she came over on the bus for a visit.

Eli and Marla were having a fight when she walked into the house with Mr. and Mrs. Finkel.

"What's going on here?" asked Mrs. Finkel.

"Eli won't give me my pimple cream," complained Marla.

"Drusilla was using it," insisted Eli.

"You're nuts! She isn't even real."

Mr. Finkel grabbed the tube of pimple cream, and it squirted all over the living room.

"Now see what you made me do?" he shouted at Eli.
"Eli," said Grandma Bessie. "Who are these people?"
"They're my friends, Grandma."

Grandma Bessie told the rest of the Finkels to clean up the mess while she went for a walk with Eli and the Dimplemeyers.

Along the way, Mr. Dimplemeyer played his harmonica. Grandma Bessie covered her ears, but she did admire Drusilla's fine, long hair and was quite impressed when Trip walked across the telephone wires. She and Mrs. Dimplemeyer chatted about knitting patterns when Mr. Dimplemeyer took a break from his harmonica.

Back home she told Eli, "Honey, your friends seem very sweet, but they really do need their own place."

"You think so, Grandma?"

"Trust me, Eli," she said.

With that, the two of them marched to the big sycamore in the backyard and called for tools and lumber. Then they began sawing and hammering. By dinnertime there was a sturdy house nestled snugly in the tree's stout branches.

"What do you think?" Grandma Bessie asked Mr. Dimplemeyer.

"It will do quite nicely," he replied.

The other Dimplemeyers agreed. Eli was delighted.

As a friendly gesture, Marla painted a sign for the Dimplemeyers' new home. Mrs. Finkel baked a chocolate forest cake, and Mr. Finkel helped Eli's friends with their luggage.

In return, the Dimplemeyers invited the Finkels to dinner. While

everybody ate, Drusilla serenaded them with a rousing rendition of "Home on the Range," and Trip performed death-defying feats on the high wire. Mrs. Dimplemeyer asked Eli to give his mother some of her favorite baking recipes, which Mrs. Finkel gladly accepted.

And they all lived happily ever after.